THE MONKEY'S PAW
Stage 1

You can make three wishes. You can ask for three things in the world, and your wishes will come true. 'But this cannot happen in the modern world!' you say. Well, think about it. What can you ask for? What do you want?

When you make your wish, that is only the beginning. When you change one thing, then you change everything in the world. One change makes another. And who knows where the changes will end?

The White family in this story can make three wishes. But they make one small mistake. Their first wish comes true, then suddenly, their life is like a terrible, terrible dream.

W.W. Jacobs (1863 – 1943) was a writer of short stories. *The Monkey's Paw* is probably his most famous story.

OXFORD BOOKWORMS
Series Editor: Tricia Hedge

OXFORD BOOKWORMS

For a full list of titles in all the Oxford Bookworms series,
please refer to the *Oxford English* catalogue. Titles available include:

~ Black Series ~

Stage 1 (400 headwords)
*The Elephant Man *Tim Vicary*
*Goodbye, Mr Hollywood *John Escott*
*The Monkey's Paw *W.W. Jacobs*
*The Phantom of the Opera *Jennifer Bassett*
Under the Moon *Rowena Akinyemi*

Stage 2 (700 headwords)
*Dracula *Bram Stoker*
*New Yorkers *O. Henry* (short stories)
*Sherlock Holmes Short Stories
    Sir Arthur Conan Doyle
*Voodoo Island *Michael Duckworth*

Stage 3 (1000 headwords)
*Love Story *Erich Segal*
*The Picture of Dorian Gray *Oscar Wilde*
*Skyjack! *Tim Vicary*
Tooth and Claw *Saki* (short stories)
Wyatt's Hurricane *Desmond Bagley*

Stage 4 (1400 headwords)
*The Big Sleep *Raymond Chandler*
*The Hound of the Baskervilles
    Sir Arthur Conan Doyle
Lord Jim *Joseph Conrad*
*Three Men in a Boat *Jerome K. Jerome*

Stage 5 (1800 headwords)
Deadlock *Sara Paretsky*
*Ghost Stories *retold by Rosemary Border*
Heat and Dust *Ruth Prawer Jhabvala*
I, Robot *Isaac Asimov* (short stories)
*Wuthering Heights *Emily Brontë*

Stage 6 (2500 headwords)
*American Crime Stories *retold by John Escott*
Cry Freedom *John Briley*
Meteor *John Wyndham* (short stories)
*Pride and Prejudice *Jane Austen*
*Tess of the d'Urbervilles *Thomas Hardy*

~ Green Series ~

Stage 2 (700 headwords)
*Alice's Adventures in Wonderland *Lewis Carroll*
*Huckleberry Finn *Mark Twain*
*Robinson Crusoe *Daniel Defoe*
Too Old to Rock and Roll *Jan Mark* (short stories)

Stage 3 (1000 headwords)
*The Call of the Wild *Jack London*
On the Edge *Gillian Cross*
*The Prisoner of Zenda *Anthony Hope*
*The Secret Garden *Frances Hodgson Burnett*

Stage 4 (1400 headwords)
*Black Beauty *Anna Sewell*
*Gulliver's Travels *Jonathan Swift*
*Little Women *Louisa May Alcott*
The Silver Sword *Ian Serraillier*
*Treasure Island *Robert Louis Stevenson*

Many other titles available, both classic and modern.
**Cassettes available for these titles.*

OXFORD BOOKWORMS COLLECTION

Fiction by well-known authors, both classic and modern.
Texts are not abridged or simplified in any way. Titles available include:

From the Cradle to the Grave
    (stories by *Saki, Evelyn Waugh, Roald Dahl,*
    Susan Hill, Raymond Carver, and others)
Crime Never Pays
    (stories by *Agatha Christie, Patricia Highsmith,*
    Graham Greene, Ruth Rendell, and others)

A Window on the Universe
    (stories by *Ray Bradbury, Arthur C. Clarke,*
    Isaac Asimov, Philip K. Dick, and others)
The Eye of Childhood
    (stories by *D. H. Lawrence, William Boyd,*
    Penelope Lively, John Updike, and others)

The
Monkey's Paw

W. W. Jacobs

retold by
Diane Mowat

OXFORD UNIVERSITY PRESS

Oxford University Press
Great Clarendon Street, Oxford OX2 6DP

Oxford New York
Athens Auckland Bangkok Bogota Buenos Aires
Calcutta Cape Town Chennai Dar es Salaam Delhi
Florence Hong Kong Istanbul Karachi Kuala Lumpur
Madrid Melbourne Mexico City Mumbai Nairobi Paris
Sao Paulo Singapore Taipei Tokyo Toronto Warsaw
and associated companies in
Berlin Ibadan

OXFORD and OXFORD ENGLISH
are trade marks of Oxford University Press

ISBN 0 19 421639 X

This simplified edition
© Oxford University Press 1989

First published 1989
Fifteenth impression 1998

The publishers are grateful to the Society of Authors, as literary
representative of the Estate of W. W. Jacobs, for permission to
create this simplified edition.

Illustrated by Kevin Jones

Printed in England by Clays Ltd, St Ives plc

Chapter 1

It was cold and dark out in the road and the rain did not stop for a minute. But in the little living-room of number 12 Castle Road it was nice and warm. Old Mr White and his son, Herbert, played chess and Mrs White sat and watched them. The old woman was happy because her husband and her son were good friends and they liked to be together. 'Herbert's a good son,' she thought. 'We waited a long time for him and I was nearly forty when he was born, but we are a happy family.' And old Mrs White smiled.

It was true. Herbert was young and he laughed a lot, but his mother and his father laughed with him. They had not got much money, but they were a very happy little family.

The two men did not talk because they played carefully. The room was quiet, but the noise of the rain was worse now and they could hear it on the windows. Suddenly old Mr White looked up. 'Listen to the rain!' he said.

'Yes, it's a bad night,' Herbert answered. 'It's not a good night to be out. But is your friend, Tom Morris, coming tonight?'

Old Mr White and his son played chess.

'Yes, that's right. He's coming at about seven o'clock,' the old man said. 'But perhaps this rain . . .'

Mr White did not finish because just then the young man heard a noise.

'Listen!' Herbert said. 'There's someone at the door now.'

'I didn't hear a noise,' his father answered, but he got up from his chair and went to open the front door. Mrs White got up too and began to put things away.

Mr White said, 'Come in, come in, Tom. It's wonderful to see you again. What a bad night! Give me your coat and then come into the living-room. It's nice and warm in there.'

The front door was open, and in the living-room Mrs White and Herbert felt the cold. Then Mr White came back into the living-room with a big, red-faced man.

'This is Tom Morris,' Mr White told his wife and son. 'We were friends when we were young. We worked together before Tom went to India. Tom, this is my wife and this is our son, Herbert.'

'Pleased to meet you,' Tom Morris said.

'Pleased to meet you, Mr Morris,' Mrs White answered. 'Please come and sit down.'

'Yes, come on, Tom,' Mr White said. 'Over here. It's nice and warm.'

'Thank you,' the big man answered and he sat down.

'Let's have some whisky,' old Mr White said. 'You need something to warm you on a cold night.' He got out a bottle of whisky and the two old friends began to drink and talk. The little family listened with interest to this visitor from far away and he told them many strange stories.

Chapter 2

After some time Tom Morris stopped talking and Mr White said to his wife and son, 'Tom was a soldier in India for twenty-one years. India is a wonderful country.'

'Yes,' Herbert said. 'I'd like to go there.'

'Oh, Herbert!' his mother cried. She was afraid because she did not want to lose her son.

'I wanted to go to India too,' her husband said, 'but . . .'

'It's better for you here!' the soldier said quickly.

'But you saw a lot of strange and wonderful things in India. I want to see them too one day,' Mr White said.

The soldier put down his whisky. 'No!' he cried. 'Stay here!'

Old Mr White did not stop. 'But your stories were

4

'Let's have some whisky,' old Mr White said.

interesting,' he said to Tom Morris. 'What did you begin to say about a monkey's paw?'

'Nothing!' Morris answered quickly. 'Well . . . nothing important.'

'A monkey's paw?' Mrs White said.

'Come on, Mr Morris! Tell us about it,' Herbert said.

Morris took his whisky in his hand, but suddenly he put it down again. Slowly he put his hand into the pocket of his coat and the White family watched him.

'What is it? What is it?' Mrs White cried.

Morris said nothing. He took his hand out of his pocket. The White family watched carefully – and in the soldier's hand they saw something little and dirty.

Mrs White moved back, afraid, but her son, Herbert, took it and looked at it carefully.

'Well, what is it?' Mr White asked his friend.

'Look at it,' the soldier answered. 'It's a little paw . . . a monkey's paw.'

'A monkey's paw!' Herbert said – and he laughed. 'Why do you carry a monkey's paw in your pocket, Mr Morris?' he asked the old soldier.

'Well, you see,' Morris said, 'this monkey's paw is magic!'

Herbert laughed again, but the soldier said, 'Don't laugh, boy. Remember, you're young. I'm old now and

Herbert looked carefully at the monkey's paw.

'An old Indian gave the monkey's paw to one of my friends.'

in India I saw many strange things.' He stopped talking for a minute and then he said, 'This monkey's paw can do strange and wonderful things. An old Indian gave the paw to one of my friends. My friend was a soldier too. This paw is magic because it can give three wishes to three people.'

'Wonderful!' Herbert said.

'But these three wishes don't bring happiness,' the soldier said. 'The old Indian wanted to teach us something — it's never good to want to change things.'

'Well, did your friend have three wishes?' Herbert asked the old soldier.

'Yes,' Morris answered quietly. 'And his third and last wish was to die!'

Mr and Mrs White listened to the story and they felt afraid, but Herbert asked, 'And did he die?'

'Yes, he did,' Morris said. 'He had no family, so his things came to me when he died. The monkey's paw was with his things, but he told me about it before he died,' Tom Morris finished quietly.

'What were his first two wishes, then?' Herbert asked. 'What did he ask for?'

'I don't know. He didn't want to tell me,' the soldier answered.

For a minute or two everybody was quiet, but then

Herbert said, 'And you, Mr Morris: did you have three wishes?'

'Yes, I did,' Morris answered. 'I was young. I wanted many things – a fast car, money . . .' Morris stopped for a minute and then he said with difficulty, 'My wife and my young son died in an accident in the car. Without them I didn't want the money, so, in the end, I wished to lose it. But it was too late. My wife and my child were dead.'

The room was very quiet. The White family looked at the unhappy face of the old soldier.

Then Mr White said, 'Why do you want the paw now? You don't need it. You can give it to someone.'

'How can I give it to someone?' the soldier said. 'The monkey's paw brings unhappiness with it.'

'Well, give it to me,' Mr White said. 'Perhaps this time it . . .'

'No!' Tom Morris cried. 'You're my friend. I can't give it to you.' Then, after a minute, he said, 'I can't give it to you, but, of course you can take it from me. But remember – this monkey's paw brings unhappiness!'

Old Mr White did not listen and he did not think. Quickly, he put out his hand, and he took the paw.

Tom Morris looked unhappy, but Mr White did not want to wait.

'What do I do now?' he asked his friend.

'The monkey's paw brings unhappiness with it.'

'What can I wish for? We need money, of course.'

12

'Yes, come on, Father,' Herbert said. 'Make a wish!' And he laughed.

The soldier said nothing and Mr White asked him again, 'What do I do now?'

At first the old soldier did not answer, but in the end he said quietly, 'OK. But remember! Be careful! Think before you make your wish.'

'Yes, yes,' Mr White said.

'Take the paw in your right hand and then make your wish, but . . .' Tom Morris began.

'Yes, we know,' Herbert said. 'Be careful!'

Just then old Mrs White stood up and she began to get the dinner. Her husband looked at her. Then he smiled and said to her, 'Come on. Help me! What can I wish for? We need money, of course.'

Mrs White laughed, but she thought for a minute and then she said, 'Well, I'm getting old now and sometimes it's difficult to do everything. Perhaps I need four hands and not two. Yes, ask the paw to give me two more hands.'

'OK, then,' her husband said, and he took the monkey's paw in his right hand. Everybody watched him and for a minute he waited. Then he opened his mouth to make his wish.

Suddenly Tom Morris stood up. 'Don't do it!' he cried.

The old soldier's face was white. Herbert and his mother laughed, but Mr White looked at Tom's face.

Old Mr White was afraid and he put the monkey's paw into his pocket.

After a minute or two they sat down at the table and began to have dinner. The soldier told the family many strange and wonderful stories about India. They forgot the monkey's paw, and because the soldier's stories were interesting, they asked him many questions about India. When Tom Morris stood up to leave, it was very late.

'Thank you for a very nice evening,' Morris said to the family. 'And thank you for a very good dinner,' he said to Mrs White.

'It was a wonderful evening for us, Tom,' old Mr White answered. 'Your stories were very interesting. Our life isn't very exciting and we don't have the money to visit India, so please come again soon. You can tell us some more stories about India.'

Then the old soldier put on his coat. He said goodbye to the White family, and went out into the rain.

The soldier told the family many stories about India.

Chapter 3

It was nearly midnight. In their warm living-room, the two old people and their son sat and talked about the soldier's stories.

'India is a wonderful country,' Mr White said. 'What exciting stories! It was a good evening.'

Mrs White stood up to take some things into the kitchen, but she stopped and listened to Herbert and his father.

'Yes,' Herbert said. 'Morris told some interesting stories, but, of course, some of them weren't true.'

'Oh Herbert!' Mrs White said.

'Well, Mother, that story about the monkey's paw wasn't true. A dirty little monkey's paw isn't magic! But it was a good story.' And Herbert smiled.

'Well, I think you're right, Herbert,' his mother said.

'I don't know,' Mr White said quietly. 'Perhaps the story was true. Strange things can happen sometimes.'

Mrs White looked at her husband. 'Did you give some money to Tom Morris for that paw?' she asked. 'We don't have money to give away for nothing!' Mrs White was angry now.

'Well, yes,' her husband answered. 'I did, but not

'Perhaps the story was true.'

much, and at first he didn't want to take it. He wanted the monkey's paw.'

'Well, he can't have it,' Herbert laughed. 'It's our paw now and we're going to be rich and happy. Come on, Father. Make a wish!'

Old Mr White took the paw from his pocket. 'OK, Herbert, but what am I going to ask for? I have everything – you, your mother. What do I need?'

'Money, of course,' Herbert answered quickly. 'We need money! You're always thinking about money. That's because we haven't got very much of it. With money you can pay for this house. It can be your house! Go on, Father, wish for thirty thousand pounds!'

17

'I wish for £30,000.'

Herbert stopped talking and his old father thought for a minute. The room was quiet and they could hear the rain on the windows.

Then Mr White took the monkey's paw in his right hand. He was afraid, but he looked at his wife and she smiled at him.

'Go on,' she said.

Slowly and carefully Mr White said, 'I wish for thirty thousand pounds.'

Suddenly he gave a cry and Mrs White and Herbert ran to him.

'What's the matter, Father?' Herbert asked.

'It moved!' Mr White cried. 'The monkey's paw – it moved!'

18

They looked at the paw. It was now on the floor and not in the old man's hand. The family watched it, and they waited – but it did not move again.

So the little family sat down again and they waited. Nothing happened. The noise of the rain on the windows was worse now and their little living-room did not feel nice and warm.

Mrs White said, 'It's cold. Let's go to bed.'

Mr White did not answer and in the end Herbert said, 'Well, there's no money, Father. Your friend's story wasn't true.' But Mr White did not answer. He sat quietly and said nothing.

After some time Mrs White said to her husband, 'Are you OK?'

'Yes, yes,' the old man answered, 'but for a minute or two I was afraid.'

'Well, we needed that money,' Mrs White said, 'but we aren't going to get it. I'm tired. I'm going to bed.'

After Mrs White went to bed, the two men sat and smoked for some time.

Then Herbert said, 'Well, Father, I'm going to bed too. Perhaps the money is in a bag under your bed! Goodnight, Father.' And Herbert laughed and went out of the room.

Old Mr White sat in the cold living-room for a long time. The candle died and it was dark. Suddenly, the

Suddenly, he saw a face at the window.

old man saw a face at the window. Quickly, he looked
again, but there was nothing there. He felt afraid.
Slowly he stood up and left the cold, dark room.

Chapter 4

The next morning the winter sun came through the
window and the house felt nice and warm again.
Mr White felt better and he smiled at his wife and son.
The family sat down to have breakfast and they began
to talk about the day. The monkey's paw was on a

'I'm going to work,' Herbert said.

little table near the window, but nobody looked at it and nobody thought about it.

'I'm going to the shops this morning,' Mrs White said. 'I want to get something nice for dinner. Are you going to come with me?' she asked her husband.

'No, I'm going to have a quiet morning. I'm going to read,' her husband answered.

'Well, I'm not going to go out this evening,' Herbert said, 'so we can go to bed early tonight. We were very late last night.'

'And we aren't going to have stories about monkeys' paws!' Mrs White said. She was angry. 'Why did we listen to your friend?' she asked her husband. 'A monkey's paw can't give you things!' She stopped but the two men did not answer her. 'Thirty thousand pounds!' she said quietly. 'We needed that money.'

Just then Herbert looked at the clock and stood up. 'I'm going to work,' he said. 'Perhaps the postman has got the money for you in a letter. Remember, I want some of it too!' Herbert laughed and his mother laughed too.

'Don't laugh, son,' Mr White said. 'Tom Morris is an old friend and he thinks the story is true. Perhaps it is.'

'Well, leave some of the money for me,' Herbert laughed again.

His mother laughed too and she went to the door with him.

'Goodbye, Mother,' Herbert said happily. 'Get something nice for dinner this evening at the shops. I'm always hungry after a day at work.'

'I know you are!' Mrs White answered.

Herbert left the house and walked quickly down the road. His mother stood at the door for some time and watched him. The winter sun was warm, but suddenly she felt very cold.

Mrs White stood at the door for some time.

Chapter 5

Slowly, old Mrs White went back into the house. Her husband looked up and saw something strange in her face.

'What's the matter?' he asked.

'Nothing,' his wife answered, and she sat down to finish her breakfast. She began to think about Tom Morris again and suddenly she said to her husband, 'Your friend drank a lot of whisky last night! A monkey's paw! What a story!'

Mr White did not answer her because just then the postman arrived. He brought two letters for them – but there was no money in them. After breakfast the two old people forgot about the money and the monkey's paw.

Later in the day, at about one o'clock, Mr and Mrs White sat down to eat and then they began to talk about money again. They did not have very much money, so they often needed to talk about it.

'That thirty thousand pounds,' Mrs White said, 'we need it!'

'But it didn't come this morning,' her husband answered. 'Let's forget it!'

Then he said, 'But that thing moved. The monkey's paw moved in my hand! Tom's story was true!'

'You drank a lot of whisky last night. Perhaps the paw didn't move,' Mrs White answered.

'It moved!' Mr White cried angrily.

At first his wife did not answer, but then she said, 'Well, Herbert laughed about it . . .'

Suddenly she stopped talking. She stood up and went over to the window.

'What's the matter?' her husband asked.

'There's a man in front of our house,' Mrs White answered. 'He's a stranger – very tall – and well dressed.

'There's a tall, well-dressed stranger in front of our house.'

25

'Can I come in and talk to you?'

He's looking at our house . . . Oh, no . . . it's OK . . .
He's going away . . .'

'Come and sit down! Finish eating!' Mr White said.

The old woman did not listen to her husband. 'He
isn't going away,' she went on. 'He's coming back. I
don't know him – he's a stranger. Yes, he's very well
dressed . . .' Suddenly Mrs White stopped. She was
very excited. 'He's coming to the door . . . Perhaps he's
bringing the money!'

And she ran out of the room to open the front door.

The tall, well-dressed stranger stood there. For a
minute he said nothing, but then he began, 'Good
afternoon. I'm looking for Mr and Mrs White.'

'Well, I'm Mrs White,' the old woman answered.
'What can I do for you?'

At first the stranger did not answer, but then he said,
'Mrs White, I'm from Maw and Meggins. Can I come
in and talk to you?'

Maw and Meggins had a big factory and Herbert
White worked there on the machinery.

'Yes, of course,' Mrs White answered. 'Please come
in.'

The well-dressed stranger came into the little living-
room and Mr White stood up.

'Are you Mr White?' the stranger began. Then he
went on, 'I'm from Maw and Meggins.'

Mrs White looked at the stranger and she thought, 'Perhaps he has the money . . . but why Maw and Meggins? And his face is very unhappy . . . Why?' Suddenly the old woman was afraid.

'Please sit down,' Mr White began, but now his wife could not wait.

'What's the matter?' she cried. 'Is Herbert . . .' She could not finish the question.

The stranger did not look at their faces – and Mr White began to be afraid too.

'Please, tell us!' he said.

'I'm very sorry,' the man from Maw and Meggins began. He stopped for a minute and then he began again. 'I'm very sorry, but this morning there was an accident at the factory . . .'

'What's the matter? Is Herbert OK?' Mrs White cried again.

'Well . . .' the man began slowly.

'Is he in hospital?' the old woman asked, very afraid now.

'Yes, but . . .' the stranger looked at Mrs White's face and stopped.

'Is he dead? Is Herbert dead?' Mr White asked quietly.

'Dead!' Mrs White cried. 'Oh no . . . please . . . not dead! Not Herbert! Not our son!'

Suddenly the old woman stopped because she saw the stranger's face. Then the two old people knew. Their son was dead! Old Mrs White began to cry quietly and Mr White put his arm round her.

Some time later the man from Maw and Meggins said, 'It was the machinery – an accident. Herbert called, "Help!". The men heard him – and ran to him quickly, but they could do nothing. The next minute he was in the machinery. I'm very, very sorry,' he finished.

For a minute or two the room was quiet. At last Mrs White said, 'Our son! Dead! We're never going to see him again. What are we going to do without him?'

Her husband said, 'He was our son. We loved him.'

'This morning there was an accident at the factory . . .'

'Maw and Meggins want to help you at this unhappy time.'

Then Mrs White asked the stranger, 'Can we see him? Can we see our son? Please take me to him. I want to see my son.'

But the stranger answered quickly, 'No!' he said. 'It's better not to see him. They couldn't stop the machinery quickly. He was in there for a long time. And at first they couldn't get him out. He was . . .' The man stopped. Then he said, 'Don't go to see him!'

The stranger went over to the window because he did not want to see the faces of the two old people. He said nothing, but he stood there for some time and he waited.

Then he went back to the old people and began to

talk again. 'There's one more thing,' he said. 'Your son worked for Maw and Meggins for six years and he was a good worker. Now Maw and Meggins want to help you at this unhappy time.' Again the stranger stopped. After a minute he began again. 'Maw and Meggins want to give you some money.' Then he put something into Mr White's hand.

Old Mr White did not look at the money in his hand. Slowly he stood up and looked at the stranger, afraid. 'How much?' Mr White asked, very quietly. He did not want to hear the answer.

'Thirty thousand pounds,' the stranger said.

Chapter 6

Three days later, in the big, new cemetery two miles from their house, the two old people said goodbye to their dead son. Then they went back to their dark, old house. They did not want to live without Herbert, but they waited for something good to happen, something to help them. The days went by very slowly. Sometimes they did not talk because there was nothing to say without Herbert. And so the days felt very long.

Then, one night, about a week later, Mrs White got out of bed because she could not sleep. She sat by the

The two old people said goodbye to their dead son.

window and she watched and waited for her son. He did not come and she began to cry quietly.

In the dark her husband heard her and he called, 'Come back to bed. It's cold out there.'

'It's colder for my son,' his wife answered. 'He's out there in the cold cemetery.'

Mrs White did not go back to bed, but Mr White was old and tired and the bed was warm. So, in the end, he went to sleep again. Suddenly he heard a cry from his wife.

'The paw!' she cried. 'The monkey's paw!' She came back to the bed and stood there.

'What is it? What's the matter?' Mr White cried. He sat up in bed. 'What's the matter?' he thought. 'Why is she excited? What's she talking about?' He looked at his wife.

Her face was very white in the dark. 'I want it,' she said quietly, 'and you've got it! Give it to me! Please!'

'What?' Mr White asked.

'The monkey's paw,' Mrs White said. 'Where is it?'

'It's downstairs,' Mr White answered. 'Why?'

Mrs White began to laugh and cry. 'We can have two more wishes!' she cried. 'We had one – but there are two more!'

'Oh, no! Not again! Think, woman!' Mr White cried. But Mrs White did not listen.

'The monkey's paw! We can have two more wishes!'

'Quickly,' she said. 'Go and get the paw. We're going to wish for our boy to come back to us!'

'No!' Mr White cried. 'You're mad!'

'Get it! Get it quickly!' Mrs White cried again.

Mr White said again, 'Think, woman! Think! Our boy was in the machinery for a long time. They didn't want to show him to us! Think! Do you want to see his body?'

'Yes! He's my son. I'm not afraid of him!' she answered.

'You don't understand,' Mr White said sadly, but he went downstairs to look for the monkey's paw.

In the living-room it was dark and Mr White did not have a candle. Slowly, he went across the room and he

34

'I wish for my son, Herbert, to come back to us.'

put out his hand for the monkey's paw. He touched it, and quickly took his hand away again.

'No!' he thought. 'I can't! I don't want to see Herbert! His face – after he was in the machinery . . . no!'

Then he thought about his wife – and he put out his hand and took the paw.

In the bedroom his wife waited. She saw the paw in Mr White's hand and cried, 'Quick! Make the wish!'

'I can't,' Mr White answered. 'Remember – he died in the machinery!'

'Make the wish! I'm not afraid of my own son!' Mrs White cried again.

Mr White looked sadly at his wife, but he took the

paw in his right hand and said slowly, 'I wish for my son, Herbert, to come back to us.' Then he sat down in the nearest chair.

But Mrs White went over to the window and looked out into the road. She stayed there for a long time and she did not move. Nothing happened. The monkey's paw could not do it!

'Thank God!' Mr White said, and he went back to bed.

Soon Mrs White went to bed too.

Chapter 7

But they did not sleep. They waited and they listened. In the end Mr White got up to get a candle because the dark made him more afraid. He began to go downstairs, but suddenly he heard a noise at the front door. He stopped, and he listened. He could not move. Then the noise came again. This time he ran. He ran upstairs, back into the bedroom and he closed the door behind him. But again the noise came.

'What's that?' Mrs White cried, and she sat up in bed.

'Nothing! Go to sleep again!' her husband answered.

But Mrs White listened – and the noise came again.

'The paw!' Mr White thought. 'Where's the monkey's paw?'

'It's Herbert! It's Herbert!' she cried. 'I'm going to open the door for him.'

And she got out of bed and ran to the door of the bedroom. Mr White got there first and stopped her.

'No!' he cried. 'Think!'

'But it's my boy! It's Herbert,' she answered.

'No! Don't go! Don't . . .' her husband cried again.

But Mrs White did not listen to him. She opened the bedroom door and ran from the room. 'I'm coming, Herbert. I'm coming!' she called.

Mr White ran after her. 'Stop!' he cried. 'Remember, Herbert died in the machinery! You don't want to see him!'

For a minute Mrs White stopped and looked at her husband, but then the noise came again and she began to run downstairs.

'Help me! Help me!' she called to her husband.

But Mr White did not move. 'The paw!' he thought. 'Where's the monkey's paw?'

He ran back into the bedroom. 'Quick!' he thought. 'Where is it?' At first he could not find it in the dark. Ah! There it was! He had it!

Just at that minute he heard his wife downstairs.

'Wait! Wait, Herbert! I'm coming!' she cried. She began to open the front door.

At the same time Mr White took the monkey's paw

The road was dark and quiet.

in his right hand and he made his third wish.

Mrs White gave a long unhappy cry and her husband ran down to her. She stood by the open door. Very afraid, old Mr White looked out into the dark.

The road was dark and quiet – and there was nobody there.

Exercises

A Checking your understanding

Chapter 1 *Write down the answers to these questions.*
1 Who lived at number 12 Castle Road?
2 What do we know about the people in the family?

Chapter 2 *Write the answers to these questions.*
1 How long was Tom Morris in India?
2 Why did the soldier not want to talk about the monkey's paw?
3 Why was the paw magic?
4 How did the monkey's paw bring unhappiness to Tom Morris?

Chapters 3 and 4 *Are these sentences true (T) or false (F)?*
1 Mr White gave Tom Morris some money for the monkey's paw.
2 Mr White gave a cry because the monkey's paw moved.
3 Mr and Mrs White went to bed and Herbert sat and smoked.
4 At breakfast the White family sat and talked about the monkey's paw.
5 Mrs White did not want the thirty thousand pounds.

Chapter 5 *Write down the answers to these questions.*
1 What do we know about the man who came to the house?
2 Why do you think the stranger said, 'It's better not to see him.'?
3 How did Mr White feel when the stranger gave him the money?

Chapter 6 *Write down the answers to these questions.*
1 How were Mr and Mrs White different after Herbert died?
2 Why did Mrs White want the monkey's paw again?
3 Why did Mr White not want Herbert to come back?

Chapter 7 *Are these sentences true (T) or false (F)?*
1 Mr White got a candle from the room downstairs.
2 Mr and Mrs White heard a noise in the street.

3 Mr White wanted his wife to open the front door.
4 Mr White took the monkey's paw in his left hand and made his third wish.

B Working with language

1 *Complete these sentences with information from the story.*
1 The White family liked Tom's stories because . . . . .
2 When Mr White first wished for the money he . . . . .
3 Herbert wanted to go to India because . . . . .
4 Mr White felt afraid because . . . . .
5 Mr White ran into the bedroom and closed the door because . . . . .
6 Mrs White ran downstairs because . . . . .
7 Herbert did not come back because . . . . .

2 *Here are some beginnings and endings of some sentences from chapters 1 and 2. Can you put them together?*

1 The two men did not talk	7 when we were young.
2 We were friends	8 to this visitor from far away.
3 Give me your coat	9 because it can give three wishes to three people.
4 The little family listened with interest	
5 This paw is magic	10 and then make your wish.
6 Take the paw in your right hand	11 because they played carefully.
	12 and then come into the living room.

C Activities

1 You are the man from Maw and Meggins. Write his diary for the day when he visited Mr and Mrs White.
2 Tom Morris comes back to 12 Castle Road after Herbert is dead. What does he say to Mr and Mrs White, and what do they say to him?
3 You have three wishes. What do you ask for, and why?

Glossary

began past tense of 'to begin'
brought past tense of 'to bring'
came past tense of 'to come'
candle something to give light
cemetery where we put a dead person in the ground
chess two people play this game with black and white 'men' (see the picture on page 2)
could past tense of 'can'
cried past tense of 'to cry'
factory a place where workers make things
felt past tense of 'to feel'
forgot past tense of 'to forget'
go on not stop
got past tense of 'to get'
had past tense of 'to have'
happiness being happy
heard past tense of 'to hear'
idea when you think of something new
Indian (*n*) a person from India
kitchen the room where you cook food
left (*v*) past tense of 'to leave'
living-room the room where you sit and talk
machinery machines which make things in a factory
mad ill in the head
magic something which can do wonderful things
monkey a small animal with a long tail (see the picture on the front cover)
paw the hand or foot of an animal
pay give money for something
put away put things where they were before
sad not happy
said past tense of 'to say'

sat past tense of 'to sit'
saw past tense of 'to see'
show to let someone see
soldier a man who fights for his country
stood past tense of 'to stand'
strange different, not known
sun the yellow sun in the sky gives us light and heat
Thank God! we say these words when we are happy because something bad has not happened
thought (*v*) past tense of 'to think'
together with somebody
told past tense of 'to tell'
took past tense of 'to take'
touch put your hand or finger on something
unhappy not happy
whisky a strong drink from Scotland
wish (*v*) want
wish (*n*) saying what you want